PENGUIN BOOKS

MISS REMARKABLE AND HER CAREER

Joanna Rubin Dranger lives in Stockholm and works as a writer and an illustrator She received the Swedish Illustrators' Award in 2000, for Best Graphic Novel for "Miss Remarkable and her Career", with the praise: "...with charm, intelligence and humour, she is able to portray the nuances of our everyday life." "Miss Remarkable and her Career" is her second graphic novel, following the successful "Miss Scardey-Cat and Love". She has also published two illustrated books for children.

Joanna Rubin Dranger

Miss Remarkable
&
Her Career

Translated by Maura Tavares

PENGUIN BOOKS

PENGUIN BOOKS

Published by the Penguin Group

Penguin Group (USA) Inc., 375 Hudson Street, New York, New York 10014, U.S.A.
Penguin Books Ltd, 80 Strand, London WC2R 0RL, England
Penguin Books Australia Ltd, 250 Camberwell Road, Camberwell, Victoria 3124, Australia
Penguin Books Canada Ltd, 10 Alcorn Avenue, Toronto, Ontario, Canada M4V 3B2
Penguin Books India (P) Ltd, 11 Community Centre, Panchsheel Park, New Delhi – 110 017, India
Penguin Books (N.Z.) Ltd, Cnr Rosedale and Airborne Roads, Albany, Auckland, New Zealand
Penguin Books (South Africa) (Pty) Ltd, 24 Sturdee Avenue, Rosebank, Johannesburg 2196, South Africa

Penguin Books Ltd, Registered Offices:
80 Strand, London WC2R 0RL, England

This translation first published in Penguin Books 2003

1   3   5   7   9   10   8   6   4   2

Originally published in Swedish as *Fröken Märkvärdig och Karriären* by
Albert Bonniers Förlag, AB, Stockholm. English translation by Maura Tavares.
This edition published by arrangement with Albert Bonniers Förlag, AB, Stockholm.

Photo of Courtney Love, Copyright © Sjöberg Classic Picture
Photo of Madonna, Copyright © Jonas Ekströmer/Pressens Bild/Retna Ltd.

LIBRARY OF CONGRESS CATALOGING IN PUBLICATION DATA
Rubin Dranger, Joanna, 1970–
[Fröken Märkvärdig & karriären. English]
Miss Remarkable & her career / Joanna Rubin Dranger ; translated by Maura Tavares.
p.   cm.
ISBN 0 14 20.0300 X
I. Title: Miss Remarkable and her career.   II. Tavares, Maura.   III. Title.
PN6790.S883R8313 2003
741.5'9485—dc21   20022193069

Printed in the United States of America

To
Oivvio

"It was something she should have lived, something other than this. There is a path somewhere that she doesn't find. It is and it isn't her own fault."

Alberte and Liberty, Cora Sandel

prologue

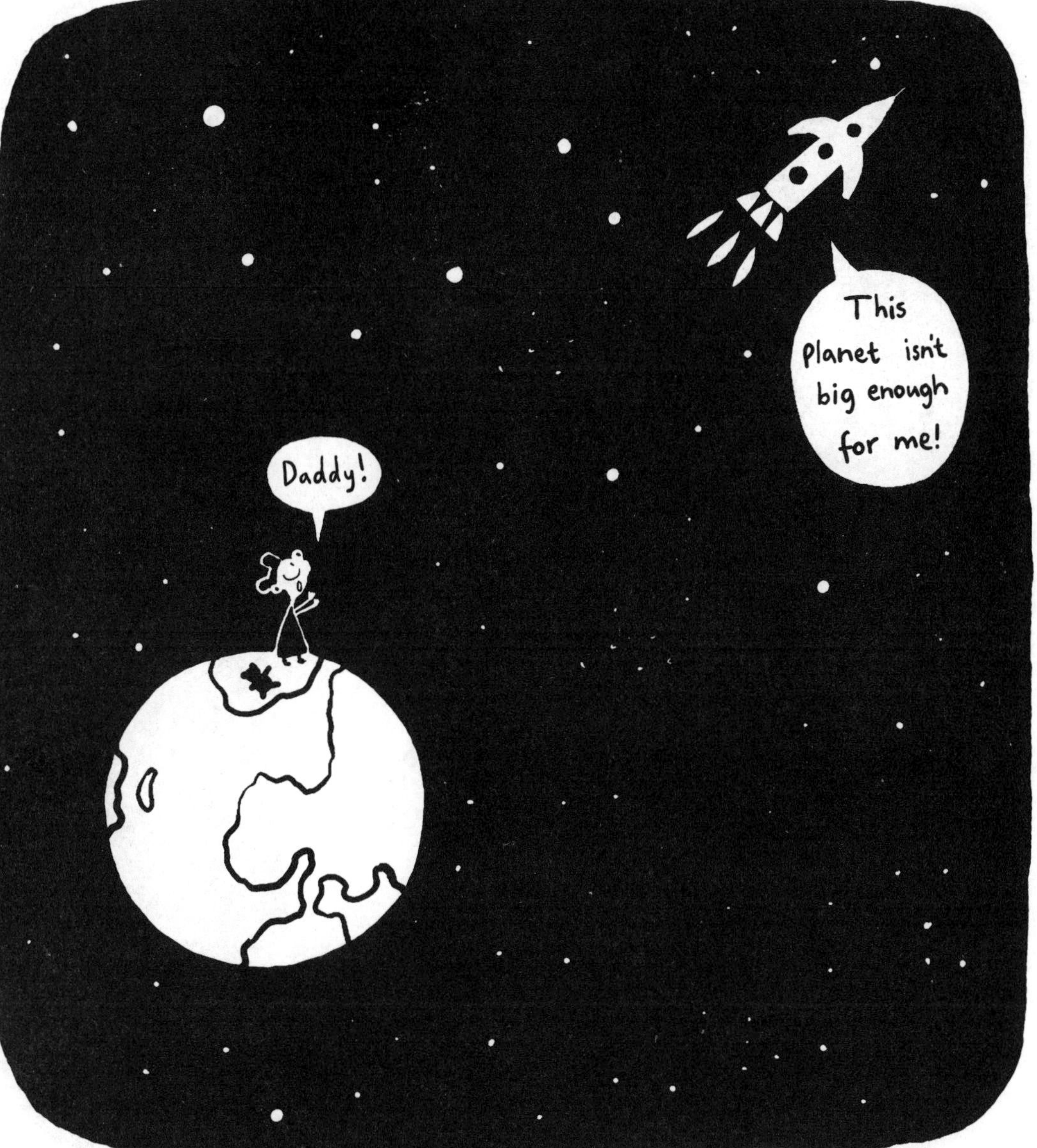
This planet isn't big enough for me!
Daddy!

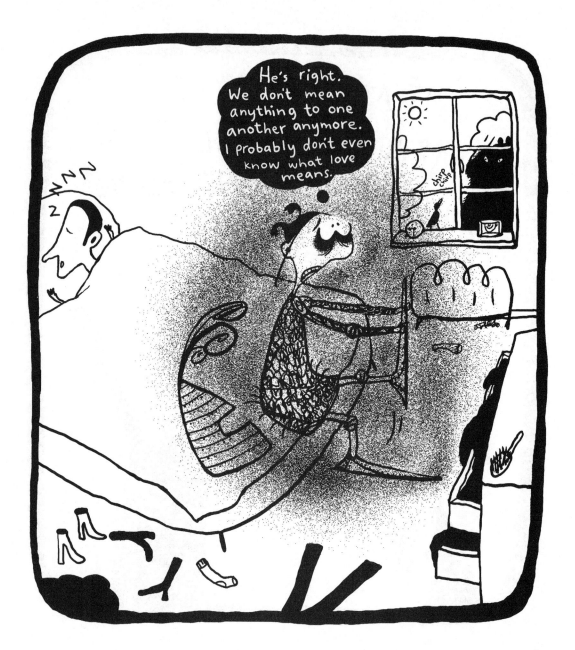

Chapter 2

Now everything's All Right.

Please come back! My life is meaningless without you!
Listen, I haven't got time for this stuff.
Just pull yourself together!
Bye, so long!

CO & MAGAZINES
STAY LIG
believe in yourself
HAPPY
PROZAC
Harries Bazaar
Strong & Pretty
Career
Success
THE FUN
10 STEPS TO BETTER SELF-ESTEEM
GET FAMOUS - all the trix!
Reach your goals
Lady
SLIM IN 10 DAYS
Cool this winter
I guess it must have something to do with some childhood repression!

Chapter 3

The loser standing small.

Oh Lord!
GOING HOME TO BED ON A WORKING DAY !!!
IT'S IM-POSSIBLE
TO BE SO WEAK!
HOOOOT !!!
chirp chirp
lalala lalala
She demands too much of life.
SHAME ON YOU!
She really must make up her mind!
Right
Who does she think she is ???
TRAGIC
You've got no valid reason to feel low!
PATHETIC
PULL YOURSELF TOGETHER

ACCORDING TO YOU IT PROBABLY LEADS TO HELL
BUT I'M NOT LISTENING TO YOU ANYMORE! Lately I've started listening to MYSELF, you see!

But Darling! I don't UNDER-STAND how it got like this! You were so sweet and happy when you where a baby!
EXHIBIT A

Heh
HEH
THE PRESS
RAPED ON
DESERTED
ISLAND
The Paper
YOUNG
WOMAN
QUARTERED
Creak
Croak
CREEEAK
CREAK
creak
Creak
Croak
Creeeak
KROAK

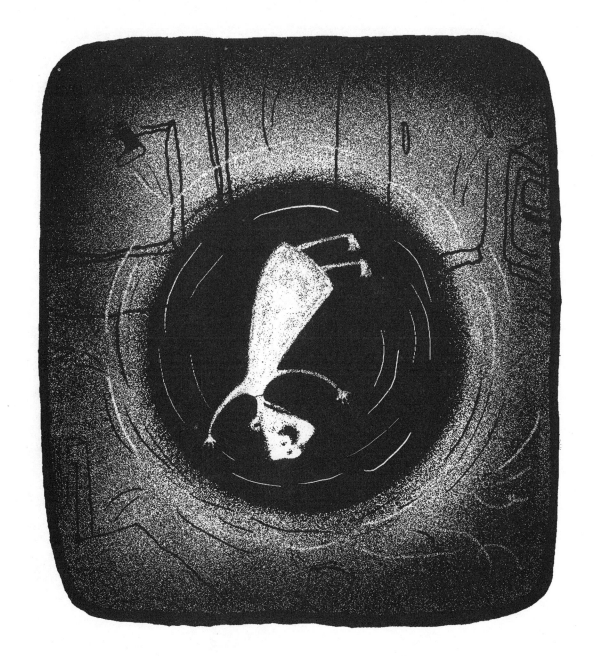

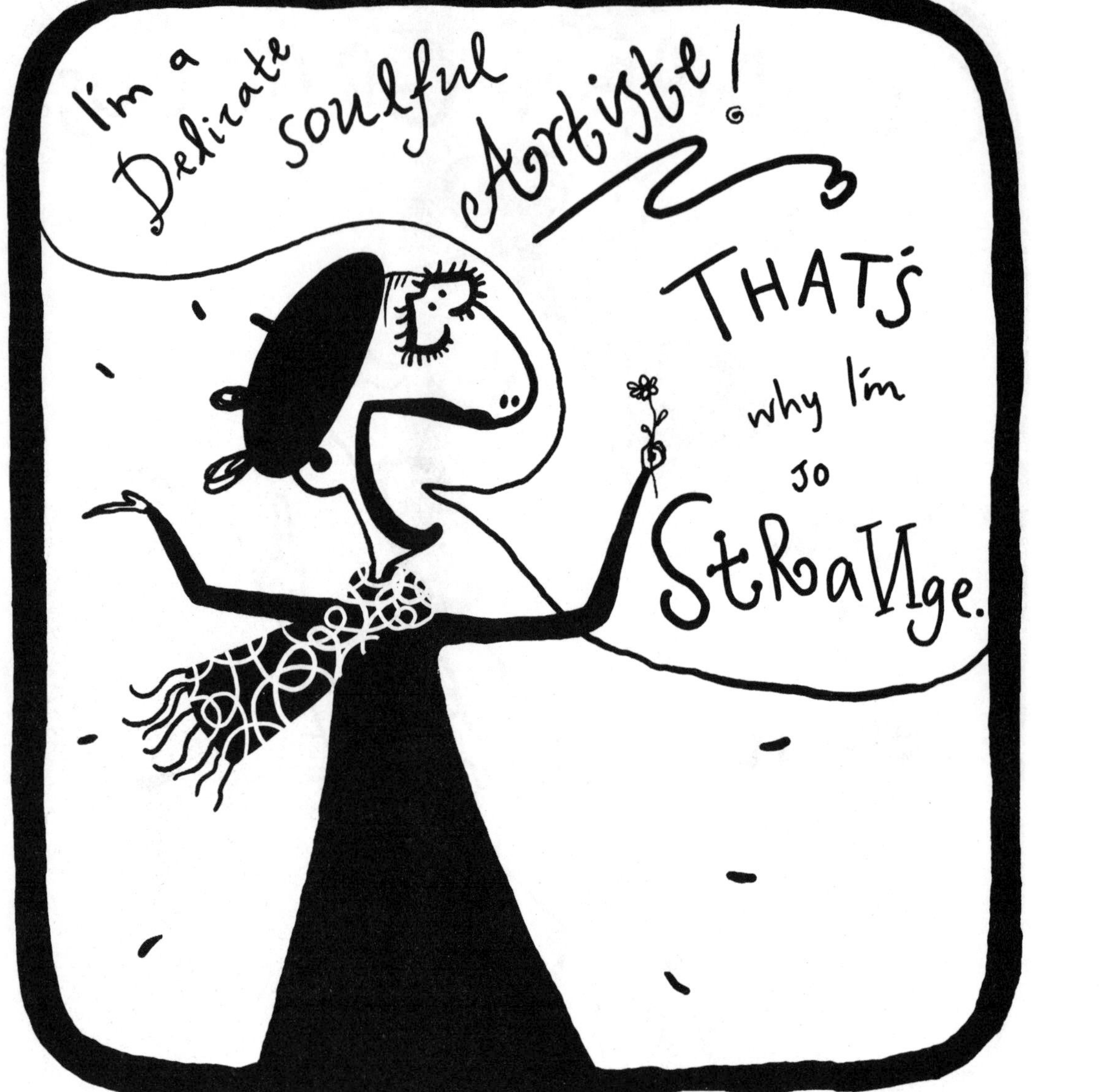
I'm a Delicate soulful Artiste!
THAT'S why I'm so StRaNge.

Our mission is to describe people to them-selves!
BRAVO
BRAVO!
HURRAH!

Ah!
A young woman's path from sorrow and misery to inner strength and success!
grunt grunt
Brilliant! Original!

NOTHING?
THEN THAT'S IT.
THE COURT HEREBY SENTENCES YOU TO A LIFETIME OF SHAME AND ISOLATION!

Pits of worthlessness
Cause all my value as a human being is determined by my achievements!
And why do you think you feel this way?

Get a grip on yourself! What are you doing? You've got to help me! I can't handle all of this on my own!
Grrrrrr
Growl
PLing plong
Ahhrr
Grrrr

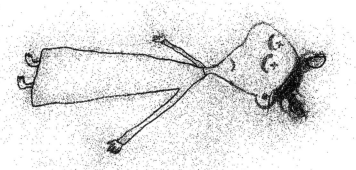

oh

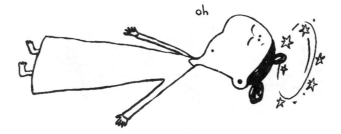

I'll
be damned.

I
do know what
I
want.

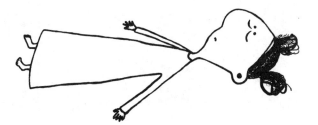

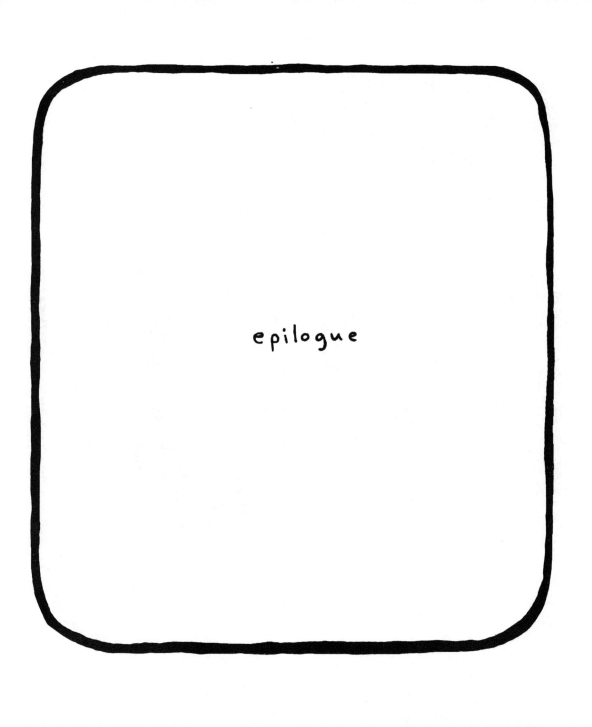

epilogue

The End